A Christmas Tale from Freedom Tavern

A Novelette

With Christmas Traditions of Burke County
Then and Now

From the Tales of Freedom Tavern Series

Patricia Cooper Baker

Patricia Cooper Baker

Tales of Freedom Tavern Series

Book 1 - *Virginia Rose and the Tory Wars*. The John Cooper family survives the hardships of 1780 North Carolina, including Tory skirmishes and the coming of the Overmountain Men as they travel toward the Battle of King's Mountain.

Book 2 – *The Way I See It* – Young Joseph Cooper finds ways to battle with Tories across North Carolina in 1780 and beyond.

Book 3 – *1784: The Birth of Morgan Towne*. The Cooper family adjust to the changes brought about by the end of the Revolutionary War and the growing township of Burke County.

Book 4 – *The Ghosts of Snakeroot Cove*. The Cooper family faces more changes brought via an encounter with an enslaved boy and his mother, living isolated in Burke County's forests in 1784.

Novelette –*When Ginny Cooper and her brother, Joe, went in search of holly and mistletoe, they were in for one of the darkest nights of their lives. It would take a miracle to bring them home.*

Copyright © 2021 Cooper's Peak, Publisher
2nd Edition: All rights reserved.
ISBN: 978-1-7359250-1-1
Library of Congress Control Number: 2020925637

Christmas with the Cooper Family

I learned about my Cooper ancestors, partly from the records that exist of their lives and times. However, I know them better from walking the fields and forests where they walked, sharing those familiar Cooper smiles, and listening to the arguments they made and the stories they told.

The Christmas traditions of my youth and those of my Grandfather were not identical, but the holiday spirit we shared was very much the same. Embrace the season, delight your family and friends, spread joy, love, and compassion.

I believe that spirit reaches back to the Burke County of the 1780s. Historical research tells me when and how the Coopers may have celebrated, but heart, soul, and family ties tell me how they felt.

Here is a story that might have been, based on love that is strong now and was vibrant even two centuries ago.

Patricia Cooper Baker

Special Thanks

To the Cooper family members who have assisted me in writing this book and others in the Tales of Freedom Tavern Series. Virginia Rose portrayed by Colby Greene, Joe Cooper by Kaden Greene, Oat Fogel by Robert Martin of Davidson Historical Park. Photography by Jane Franklin Cooper and Carol Martin.

Contents

Patricia Cooper Baker

1780s Christmas: The Season

Who wouldn't want Christmas to last a whole month?

*In the 18th century, the Christmas season may have begun on December 25, but depending on the community, it might not end until early February. For those living in English Crown colonies, such as Virginia, the season extended over the twelve days of Christmas, from the new Christmas on December 25 until the traditional Christmas date of January 6. Denominations differed on whether to celebrate Christmas on the old or the new date. The last day of the twelve, the Feast of the Epiphany, is the **real** Christmas for some groups now, and even more recognized it by that name in the 1780s.*

The most ardent of observants held religious and traditional events throughout this period, with Twelfth Night being a particularly lucky night for parties and weddings.

Since the Cooper family had Virginia roots, they probably celebrated Christmas for up to twelve days.

1 - The Day after Christmas

Virginia Rose Cooper

'Twas only the second day of Christmas, and our entire family bustled through the tavern preparing trimmings, tastes, and trappings for holiday cheer. Papa's coin box and bottles jingled as he measured the spirits for his rum punch—a full measure poured for a man's first taste of the season, and half as much went into a bowl for the ladies and any others who might ask for seconds.

"Ginny, see if your mother has tea cakes ready if you will. No visitor will leave our home without a hearty welcome, a sweet treat, and a drop of good cheer."

7

"But, who will come, Papa? The Presbyterians aren't celebrating."

"Oh, I would not wager on that. Besides, it matters little who may come, Daughter. 'Tis impossible to waste Christmas joy. Happiness brought and bounty shared makes the winter warmer for everyone."

"But the Reverend Templeton didn't even mention the birth of Jesus in yesterday's sermon."

"No, but he spoke of bringing light in dark times by sharing with others. 'Tis the time of year when magic springs from the darkness. Each man finds a way of his own to mark the season. I dare say even the staunchest Presbyterian would not hesitate to share a dram of whiskey when 'tis offered by a friend."

Papa set the spirits bottles on the counter and arranged the holly sprigs around them. He carried more greenery and berries to the mantle, where he stuffed them into vases of laurel boughs that sat on either side of his fiddle. Smiling, he reached for the bow; then, with a shake of his finger, he lay it back again.

"We must sing as we work if we want music," he said. "Tonight will be soon enough for playing a tune."

He turned back to the spirits counter and rubbed his chin as he judged his merry decoration. Flickering flames reflected off the green bottle glass and into Father's eyes.

"This time of year, I recall my boyhood Christmases when I was an Anglican in Virginia with Mother, Father, and my brother Joseph. We gathered with my grandparents and all the aunts,

8

uncles, and cousins. Such a time we had—one I would not want my children to miss. There are those around here happy to stir their own warm memories by dropping by for our version of an old Virginia Christmas."

While Papa's eyes were still bright from the memories, he turned to me with a wink and a smile and pointed to the kitchen. "The tea cakes if you please, Daughter, and ask your good mother where she hid those spare candles."

I hurried with the Ginger Drops and then back to my mother, sister, and the cheeriness of our Christmas kitchen. We three cooks sang at the top of our lungs while keeping time with our chopping and stirring. The joyful noise we made drowned out the boiling, bubbling, and sizzling, but the savory scent of venison roasting and the fruity perfume of Mama's persimmon and hickory nut bread trumpeted news of the coming feast to anyone in sniffing range of the kitchen.

"This batch is done. Make room," Mary Jane called. She slid the first golden loaf from the fireplace oven to her wooden paddle and spun on her heel to set it on the cooling rack.

As my sister danced from fire to table, I cracked the shutters to bring a breath of crisp air to the room. Two shadows pushed a sled past the window.

"Joe and Oat Fogel are back from the woods."

Mama and my sister nodded at the news, and the three of us continued our song as Mother wrapped the cooled loaves in paper, and I sugared the tops of the ones fresh from baking.

My brother, Joe, kicked open the door as he juggled a bundle of firewood in his arms. Hot kitchen air meeting the winter chill spread thick fog over the doorstep, but Joe's bellowing addition to "God Rest Ye Merry Gentlemen" was loud and clear. Mother rushed Joe inside and shut the door to preserve the cooking temperatures.

"Did you bring more pine boughs and laurel branches? Did you find mistletoe?" she asked.

"Oat filled this load to the brim with what the remains of that pine tree. Besides, Christmas was yesterday; do we truly need more trimmings?"

"We will have callers throughout the season, Joe. 'Tis our Christian duty to spread good cheer with our hospitality," Mary Jane replied.

Joe brushed chips of pine bark from his gloves and coat. "Well, Oat Fogel sure ain't cheerful today, and I don't reckon I can get him back out on another trip to the woods. He vowed to spend tonight alone. Snow clouds are clabbering up, too."

"Mama, may I take one of these loaves to Oat's campfire?" I asked. "The smell alone should lift his spirits."

"We will surely save a loaf for Oat, but I need you here for a while longer. Now, dust the top..." Bells jingling from the yard interrupted Mother's instructions.

"'Tis Annie!" Joe called. He and I ran to the hitching post to greet our sister and her husband, David.

"Best of the season to you," David shouted while Annie wrapped her arms around us. They hurried into the warmth of the tavern while Joe tended their horse and cart, and I helped with the parcels.

David assisted Father in the tavern room, and the cooks paused their singing long enough to welcome Annie home.

My older sister's smiling face added even more warmth to our kitchen, and she soon took over my job of sugaring loaves. We shared stories and gossip from our neighbors, but that news reminded Annie of something more serious.

"Is all well, here? When we stopped in the town, Deputy McDowell warned us of Indian sightings."

"There's been no such word on this side of the river," Mother replied.

"No signs of trouble in the woods," Joe added.

"'Tis a relief to hear that." Annie turned to the loaves once more.

"Mother, since Annie is here to help, may I take a loaf to Oat now?"

She looked over the bread and chose her smallest loaf for Oat and his lonely camp.

"Wear your boots, daughter."

"I've outgrown them," I replied.

"Wear mine then," Annie said. "I won't need them before you get back. They may be big on you, but they'll keep your feet warm and dry."

"They will be fine," I said with a grin. "I'm wearing two pairs of socks."

"Then hurry, Daughter. We have much to do before Papa and I make deliveries to our friends who can't attend tonight's feast."

1780s Christmas: Religious Differences

Roman Catholics, Lutherans, Moravians, and Anglicans have never paused in their celebration of Christmas, but in some American colonies, Christmas was not celebrated at all. In fact, parts of Puritan New England banned the observance for twenty years.

In 1659, a Massachusetts proclamation deemed the observation of Christmas as a sacrilege and that the "exchanging of gifts and greetings, dressing in fine clothing, feasting, and similar Satanical practices" were forbidden liable to a fine of five shillings. Lucky for those folks, the ban was lifted in 1681.

Things were never quite so harsh in the South. In the English Crown colonies, Anglicanism was the state religion, and celebrating Christmas was embraced. The Revolutionary War complicated things—after all, we weren't English any longer. Anglicans became Episcopalians, and celebrations carried on.

However, there was another wrinkle. Many new protestant denominations frowned upon frivolity. Others objected to the choice of the date for the birth of Jesus, and still others found some of the traditions of Christmas, customs predating the birth of Christ, to be too pagan. Quakers rejected Christmas altogether, but Baptists officially began observing Christmas in 1772, at least through religious services.

In the early days of our nation, The Presbyterians tried to ignore Christmas, but they reconsidered when their members celebrated at Episcopal services. Scots-Irishmen populating the colonies brought their traditions for Twelfth Night that blended right in with other Colonial holiday festivities.

2 - Oat Fogel

In only ten steps from the kitchen door, a chill wind bit through my cloak. I pulled the wool wrap tightly around the loaf and close to my body as I crossed the farmyard and passed the stables. The way was downhill from there, and I picked my steps to avoid the remnants of ice dotting the path to Oat's fire. The wind carried notes from a mournful flute that blended with the voices from the kitchen. But as I drew closer to the camp, the pipe and the whistling wind swallowed the carols until there was only flute song in the air.

The deep, clear notes became louder as I approached but stopped still when Oat noticed my arrival. He kept his seat but held out one hand to take the bread. He lay the loaf beside him and pointed me to a stump seat. Then the old peddler, so long a part of our household, returned to his sorrowful tune.

"Mama thanks you for bringing the firewood," I said. Oat nodded and continued playing.

"She wants Joe to go back to the woods for green trimmings for the house. Will you go with him?"

Oat finished his song before replying, "Not tonight, young lady." He glanced up at the rainbow grackle painted on his van. Then he began a new tune slower, louder, and more sorrowful than the last.

"Such a sad tune," I said. "Is it a Christmas song you play?"

"'Tis what passed for one for my wife and me," he replied. "In the long nights of winter, I especially miss my Cheenuh. When I play the old melodies, she comes to me whispering Tuscarora tales, and the spicy taste of her jugged rabbit tingles on my tongue once more."

"You say her spirit is with you everywhere ... that she comes with the birds."

The old man nodded. "She is here tonight." He continued his song.

"If you go with Joe to fetch the boughs, the job will be done before dark," I said.

The old peddler's eyes softened as he turned to me. "Tonight, I want to be with Cheenuh—at least with my memories of her. Joe can gather the boughs alone this time."

Oat turned again to his mournful songs, and I made my way back to the porch step where Joe was preparing the sled for one more venture to the woods.

"Oat isn't coming," I said.

"I didn't reckon he would," Joe replied. "He's been sullen and pouty all day—can't get past thinking of his wife, as near as I can see. He pointed out every grackle in the woods."

"We should cheer him up, Joe," I said. "If Mama and Papa are bringing bread and company to those less fortunate, we should do something right here at home to make Oat feel better."

"How are we supposed to cheer him? I don't reckon we can bring back a wife who was long dead before we ever knew him."

"He's dwelling on her flute songs and Tuscarora tales."

"Can't help none with that, neither," Joe said.

"Well, how about a rabbit for dinner? She used to make that for him. Reckon there are any rabbits in your gums, Joe?"

"Last I checked them gums, there was nary a rabbit in 'em. Some of 'em were sprung, too. We've either got a smart rabbit or a poacher stealing from my traps. There ain't much chance of finding a rabbit there."

I took two steps closer to the porch. "You don't think it could it be that Indian Annie spoke of robbing your traps?"

Joe chuckled, "Don't be daft, girl. Me and Oat would have seen signs if there was Indians in the woods. No Indians, but no rabbits today, neither."

"But you could look, again," I said. "Maybe the rabbits came back for more of your bait."

"Ginny, I have no time to walk along that thicket again today. The night will fall quickly with these clouds coming in. 'Twill be all I can do to load this sled with laurel and mistletoe and get back before dark."

"There must be something we can do for him." I bit my lip and tapped my chin, studying on how to help Oat.

Joe shook his head and muttered, "Girls... You ain't never satisfied handling the problem at hand." I glared at Joe, and his eye took on a gleam. With half a smile, he asked, "Do you want to come along to the woods with me, Ginny?"

I did *not*. Even in my father's company, I took no joy in walking through a forest where there were more wild animals than people. There might be Indians there, too—scalping Indians—like the ones that attacked Mrs. Brank.

"Mama needs me here," I replied.

"Not anymore, she don't," Joe said, "Annie and David are here to help at the tavern. Come with me. You can check the traps while I gather the greenery."

Joe awaited my answer, and I dug my toes deep into the snow, hoping I would dig up an excuse.

"I reckon you don't truly mean to spread cheer, do you, Ginny?" Joe asked. "At least, not if it causes you inconvenience. Are you only kind when 'tis easy?"

I glared at Joe while I pulled at the drawstring of my cloak so that the hood fit closer to my ears.

"Come on," he said. "I can use an extra pair of hands. I'll even give you a knife to hold if that makes you feel safer. Oat ain't gonna get no rabbits tonight if you don't come to help me."

Oat's flute melody still wafted over the farmyard, and the lamentation of that tune near brought me to tears.

"All right, Joe. I'll go with you, but we better find a rabbit in those traps."

Mother and Father emerged from the tavern, laden with packages of bread and cheese for the neighbors.

"'Tis time for us to be on our way," Mama said as she jostled her packages and handed the top one to Papa.

"David is manning the spirit's counter," Papa replied, "and Annie will be enough help with the cooking and decorating."

"She will soon need that greenery, though," Mama added.

"We're on our way to fetch that now," Joe said.

"Ginny is going with you, then?" Papa asked as he loaded the parcels into his cart.

"Aye, she'll have an eye for good mistletoe, I reckon," Joe replied.

Papa raised an eyebrow as he considered the plans of his two youngest children. Joe, stocky and nearly as muscular as a man, had proven himself as a survivor of many scrapes. As for me, well, I was two years older than Joe, and that had to count for something.

"Joe, do you have your hatchet and knife?" he asked.

My brother put his hand to his belt. "Of course, I do, Papa. Can't get mistletoe without that."

"Ginny, you tend to let your imagination fly, but you can reason, too. Keep your wits about you."

"I promise, Papa."

"The sun, what there is of it, will set early tonight. Go on and be back before dark."

Papa snapped the reins, and my parents started on their rounds to deliver their gifts of comfort and cheer. Papa turned as they reached the edge of the yard. "Use your heads—both of you," he called. "And stay within sight of each other."

Joe pushed the sled forward over the spotty ice, and the two of us trudged our way toward the shadowy woods.

1780s Holiday Fun

Some observed Christmas kept to family celebrations and church services, and others hosted parties, hunts, visiting, and feasts. Phifer claims that in Burke County, the season was active with celebration in the town of Morganton, on the plantations, and especially among the Episcopalians.

Hymns and carols, music and dancing were popular, too. Isaac Watts (1674-1748) changed religious music for his age and all the ages that followed. He left us with 750 hymns, including the carol, **Joy to the World**. The English also enjoyed Christmas songs still popular today, including **The First Noel, God Rest Ye Merry Gentlemen, The Holly and the Ivy, I Saw Three Ships,** and **Coventry Carol.** Hymns or not, you can't put a fiddle in the hands of a backwoodsman without setting toes to tapping.

The Twelve Days of Christmas was published in England in 1780, but it may not have reached the backwoods by then. The tune we are familiar with today didn't become attached to the rhyme until 1909. One source suggests that Twelve Days was a parlor game in which the twelve players name the gifts, but the ones who follow must remember all the gifts named in the game before.

While many of these traditions originated in England and Germany, the Scots-Irish had holiday traditions of their own. The border Scots brought customs of Old Christmas, including feasts, bonfires, and the firing of muskets.

The Scots also enjoyed a game of **Shinty** at Christmas. The game has evolved into something like field hockey, but the earliest versions involved one team tossing a ball at a target (milk stool was the tradition), and the other team defending the target with a bat.

1780s Christmas: Jugged Rabbit

Jugged hare (or rabbit) used a cooking technique to make this wild animal more tender and flavorful. The recipe is found in the best-selling recipe book of the 18th century: **The Art of Cookery Made Plain and Easy**, *written by Hannah Glasse in 1747.*

The cleaned rabbit was prepared for cooking by cutting it into small pieces and 'larding.' Larding involved pushing small pieces of fat (Glasse suggested bacon) into the rabbit meat. Rabbit is a low-fat wild game, and more fat was needed for texture and flavor.

The rabbit was placed in an earthenware or ceramic cooking pot (the jug), and seasonings were added: salt, pepper, mace (or nutmeg), some sweet herbs such as marjoram or rosemary, and a peeled onion spiked with cloves.

The pot was sealed with a lid pasted to the pot with dough or a membrane covering the pot to keep the steam inside. The pot was then placed into a larger vessel big enough to hold water at a depth nearly to the top of the rabbit pot. The larger crock was hung over the fire for three hours, and at the end of the cooking time, the herbs were removed, and the hot meat plated

3 - In the Woods

A thick carpet of snowy ground lay under the forest canopy. Joe chose unbroken snow for the sled, while I tried to step in the tracks he and Oat had made earlier. Cardinals, blue jays, and red berries made a cheerful contrast to the white branches.

"There's holly here, and I know where to find a good crop of mistletoe ahead," Joe said as he pulled the sled to a stop. "We'll have this job done in no time."

Joe whistled, and I hummed along as he selected holly sprays, and I arranged them in the sled. The singing reminded me of Oat's sad music.

"Did you ever hear Oat play that flute of his?" I asked.

Joe tilted his head and put a finger to his lips. "Not a flute, but I hear something," he whispered.

We stood listening to the quiet that comes with heavy cloud cover. Joe scanned the trees and peered deep into the forest.

"I don't hear ..."

"Shh!" he said. His eyes widened, and he pointed behind me. "Is that a bear?"

I gasped as I turned around, then I held my breath as we both listened more intently. Beyond the odd bird call, I heard small branches snapping and the crunch of the snow crust breaking. My eyes widened as I looked at my brother. "Should we run?" I whispered.

Joe glanced at my feet. "I can run, but those boots will come right off'n you if you try it."

My eyes widened, and my mouth fell open. *Would Joe leave me in the woods with a bear?*

My brother broke the snowy silence, guffawing as he pushed at my arm. "'Tis only a deer or fox, Ninny Ginny. Come on; the trap line is just up the way."

I stuck my tongue out at him and his prank, but his only response was a smirk as he took the sled handles and drove on ahead of me. When I caught up to him, he returned to my question about Oat.

"Yep, I heard Oat's flute before. I was there when he made it out of cedarwood. He told me he only ever made two others like that, and he lost 'em both." After a pause, he added, "Well, no, no ... I got that wrong. His wife took both of them flutes to carve, one with a bird and one with a deer. When she died, he buried the bird flute with her on account of her name, Cheenuh, being the Indian word for bird."

"What happened to the other flute?" I asked.

"He never said. Maybe he left it at his house back east."

As we walked on in silence, the cloud cover grew thicker, and under the canopy of pine and hemlock, 'twas as dark as dusk all around us. When we came upon a stand of laurels, Joe pointed to blackberry brambles that ran along the creek.

"There. That's the start of my gum line."

"I don't see a trap."

"They're hidden in the brambles. I spaced 'em about forty paces apart. Once you find the first one, just go along the creek till you find the next."

"You mean for me to go alone, then?"

"As I told you, I don't have the time to do my job and your'n, too. If you want rabbits, you get 'em. Holler if you find a full trap, and I'll come to get him out for you."

I looked toward the bramble line. The near-end was a good thirty yards away, and the line stretched into the shadows so that I couldn't see the far end at all. "You want me to go over there all by myself? Papa said for us to stay together."

"That ain't what he said," Joe replied. "Here, you can take my knife to cut the brambles back, but don't you lose it."

"Won't you need it to cut the laurel and mistletoe?"

"I got my hatchet," he said, pointing to a blade stuck into his belt. "You go on."

No more than ten feet away from him, I turned back. "What if I get lost?"

"Don't be daft! How in the world can you get lost following along the river?"

"Well, what if I do?"

Joe shook his head and rolled his eyes. "Just keep yourself alive long enough for me to finish my work, and I'll come to get you. Your trail won't be hard to follow in this snow."

After two more steps toward the bushes, I turned around again. "What if it gets dark? You can't follow my trail if you can't see it?"

Joe flung his arms on the sled handles and sighed. "That ain't likely to happen if you let me get on with my work."

"But if it does?"

"Make some noise. Whistle or sing a song. That will help me find you."

"And if you can't hear me?"

Joe shook his head and gave me one last word of advice. "Listen, Ginny, anybody over the age of ten knows how to get out of the woods. That creek over there by the brambles runs right to our spring house. But don't you head out nowhere as long as there's a chance I can find you. I don't want to waste time looking for you if you ain't still in the woods."

As I turned toward the brambles once more, I heard a crunch of sled runners in the snow, and Joe yelled, "Make it easy on both of us. Don't get lost."

1780s Christmas: Holiday Food

What did the new Americans eat at their holiday feast? The best they had available, of course.

During the American Revolution, imported goods were scarce, and that included rum, molasses, and sugar, but the New World was filled with riches of its own.

Vegetables were easy to preserve, and fresh game was available. Even a modest holiday table held roast turkey, venison, root vegetables, and treats baked with dried fruit. Wealthy Virginians before and after the war were known to prepare upwards of twenty dishes for the feast. Along with tea, beverages included cider, wine, rum punch, and in some cases, chocolate.

George Washington had a bleak Christmas in 1776 at Valley Forge, but in 1783, he returned to Mount Vernon. There, a lavish feast was prepared under the direction of his wife, Martha. Her Christmas Pie was a crust filled with layers of turkey, goose, hen, partridge, and pigeon seasoned with spices and covered in butter. She also had a recipe for Great Cake, which required 40 eggs, 4 pounds of butter, 4 pounds of powdered sugar, 5 pounds of fruit, and a half-pint of wine and brandy.

From **Revolutionary War Period Cookery**, we find that George Washington also enjoyed Apple-Ale Fritters and Martha's recipe for fruit cake given to her on her wedding day.

The many Scots-Irish around Morganton had their own tradition of fruitcake. The concoction of fruits, nuts, and spirits was also called Scotch Whisky Cake, Twelfth Night Cake, or Black Rum Cake.

According to descendants of the Avery family, Waightstill had a passion for bees and honey. Perhaps he enjoyed the same Honey Cake that was a favorite of John Adams.

1780s Christmas: No Christmas Tree?

What were the Christmas decorations found in an 18th-century backwoods cabin? Unless the family had German roots, there probably would not have been a Christmas tree. The first recorded Christmas tree in America appeared in Williamsburg around 1842. A German professor at **William and Mary College** decorated a tree as a treat for George Tucker's children.

According to **Burke: The History of a North Carolina County,** author Edmund Phifer, Jr. recounts an 1854 letter which mentions a tree to be 'fixed' for the children of Morganton.

Even before the 18th century, candles, lanterns, and fires lit the dark winter nights. There were old and honored traditions of greenery stuck in windows and boughs of holly, ivy, and laurel branches to add color. Anything aromatic, such as lavender, rose petals, spices and herbs freshened the air in a house closed against the cold, as well. Oranges, lemons, and pineapple were fruits too valuable to use as decorations, but a common focal point was a sprig of mistletoe to lighten hearts and spirits.

4 – *Along the Brambles*

Annie's boots slipped off my heels twice as I trudged toward the bramble line. Lucky for me, a corner of the first gum stuck out from the thorny vines. A push of the brambles showed a snare still set. No rabbit.

Within twenty paces, I found a line of footprints along the bushes. No doubt Joe left them when checking his traps. I stepped into them when I could to keep the snow from sucking Annie's boots off my feet. I counted out the paces as I moved along the brambles.

Finding the gum took more searching this time, but there it was. When I opened the trap, I found it empty. The bait was nibbled, but the animal was long gone. Maybe that critter changed his mind before the door fell shut.

As I negotiated the next forty paces, Joe's steps were harder to follow, but I discovered another set of man-sized tracks. They came out of the woods and toward the creek, and they were fresher than the ones Joe left. Maybe Oat made them while they were gathering wood.

These new tracks took a turn at the brush line and followed it for a way. 'Twas those tracks I stepped in as I hunted for the next gum. The third, fourth, and fifth traps were also empty. Two of them were still set to catch game, but the apples inside had been nibbled. I'd have my jape at Joe when we met again. He might not be as good at rigging gums as he thought.

A rustling in the bushes ahead of me sent a chill up my spine. After ducking for cover, I scanned the dim path ahead.

A shadow raced across the icy bank, and one splatter after another trailed up the creek and away from me. 'Twas a temptation to stop, but surely the creature that ran away was the deer Joe mentioned. *But was it four legs or two I heard splashing? Was it a man? Deputy McDowell's Indian?*

I tightened the drawstring of my hood around my hair then sat still as a possum until the running was too distant to hear. Then to shore up my courage, I took Joe's advice and sang a carol. No reply. No response. Time to move. The man-tracks veered from the blackberry brambles and took a heading eastward back into the forest. With no steps to follow, I clung to the brush, humming bits of carols, as I marched on, determined to brighten the season for Oat Fogel. My singing stopped when my cloak became entangled in the briars.

"Blast!" I used the knife to set myself free; then I moved ahead. Now, my song of *Joy to the*

World was faint, and the frigid air burned in my throat.

'Twas a struggle to keep from slipping with nothing to hold on to save the brambles, and 'twas even more difficult to get back on my feet once they slid out from under me.

"Dadgummit all!" I shouted as I fell into the bushes again.

The air grew more bitter, and light snow was falling. The next two traps were sprung, and at the one after that, the snow surface was rough and spattered with dark spots. *Was that blood?* 'Twas too dark to tell.

The snow fell heavier, and in the low light, it was hard to see the way in front of me, but I continued my trek. Amidst the eerie silence of falling snow, I heard twigs snapping in the woods beyond the bramble line as something stepped through the forest.

"Joe?" I called. The crackling stopped. I held my breath. *What or who was out there? Which way was it going?*

I backed away from the last trap as silently as I could, then I waited and listened. With one hand, I held Joe's knife at the ready, and the other arm linked onto a sapling to keep me from slipping. I could not keep an animal from finding my scent, but I held tight to avoid the noise of tumbling through the brush.

Keep still. *Was that a voice? Another? Was someone calling?* Listen. There was only the trickle of icy water through the half-frozen creek.

I slipped out of hiding and did my best to stay out of the creek as I crept along the bramble-covered bank. A wide, dark spot colored the snow ahead of me. If it were blood, there was too much of it to be from a rabbit kill. Beyond the dark pool, a trail of blotches stretched into the darkness. Mixed in the crisp, pine-scented air was the unmistakable stench of blood. What if it was Joe's blood?

I covered my nose with the hand that held the knife while trying not to imagine the worst. The clouds thinned as the moon rose, and a dim light filtered through the trees and onto the snow. 'Twas enough light to see farther ahead, and under a tall poplar, not twenty paces from me, lay a deer carcass. A beast hovered over it, ripping and gnawing into the flesh.

My back stiffened, and my mouth fell open, but thanks be to God, no scream came out. My eyes stayed fixed to the predator in the shadows.

Oat's rabbit could wait a day. I needed to find my brother and go home.

I forced one foot back and gasped as a dead branch snapped under my foot.

The animal raised its head, and bloody flesh dangled from the mouth of the predator. Eyes glowed yellow in the dim light before the face turned back to its feast. I knew that beast. 'Twas a panther.

I took one careful step backward, then another, each time being sure I stepped on soft snow. The cat was too busy with his meal to bother with me. I dared to turn and make my escape.

I lost one of Annie's boots as I turned and took only the time to catch it on the end of Joe's knife and keep running. The creek bank was slippery, so I chose a path inside the woods to steady myself by holding onto the trees and saplings along the way. Once deeper into the woods, I dared to stop long enough to remove the snow-caked outer sock and replace the boot.

It wasn't long before I saw the end of the bramble line, and to my right was the laurel thicket; the trail of sled runners marked the spot where I parted from Joe. The tracks, now filling in with fresh snow, skirted the thicket. Broken branches and dropped green leaves along the path proved Joe had worked here collecting laurel.

"Joe!" There was no answer from the fluttering snow.

My chest tightened, but I cinched my cloak around me and fought off the fear. By the time I reached the other end of the laurel grove, I could no longer see the sled tracks. Which way now?

"Joe! Joe, are you here?" No reply.

I wandered into the laurels, hoping to find any sign of my brother, but there was even less light under the branches. Soon I had not only lost my brother and my wet sock; my sense of direction was gone, as well. Eventually, I freed myself from the thicket with no idea of which way to go.

Use your head. That was Papa's motto. Collect yourself, observe what's around you, and use your head.

The cloud cover was heavy in most directions, and even where it was thinning, the sky offered no bearings other than the glow of the rising moon. This time of year, the moonrise was not to true east. My feet were growing numb, and my cheeks icy. Freezing in that spot was no good plan, but which way to move? I scouted for any sign or

31

reason to go one way instead of another. The rusty-hinge screech of a grackle sounded near me. I thought of Cheenuh and followed the bird's path as it soared into a tree, black against clouds back-lit by a pale moon. The silhouette showed clusters of mistletoe in the high branches of that oak. That's where Joe went. I'd go there, too.

My brother had been at the oak, for sure. The sled lay on its side at the tree's base amid harvested holly, laurel, and mistletoe. There were signs of a struggle in the snow, and someone had been dragged eastward into the woods. Joe was not the victor in that fight, or he'd be with the sled.

I set the sled aright and took a moment to sit there in the snow. No rabbit for Oat Fogel, and how could I go home without Joe? I had to do something, and I only had one path to follow—the one where Joe was likely in trouble.

1780's Cherokee and Tuscarora

Burke County and the Cherokee: *Somewhere in the decades of the past, the lands of Burke County became a buffer zone between the Catawba and the Cherokee, and there were no longer any permanent native settlements there. The natives passed through the lands along the Catawba as they traveled for hunting or trade, leaving the valley open for European settlers.*

By the 18th century, land-encroachment, disease, and social abuses were among the factors that soured the Cherokee relationship with Burke County's citizens. During the French and Indian War, the Cherokee sided with the French against the British, and during the American Revolution, the British encouraged Cherokee incursions against the settlers. Repercussions culminated in Griffith Rutherford's Cherokee Expedition, which brought devastation to nearby Cherokee towns.

The result was fear and distrust between the Europeans and the Cherokee people during the harsh times in which this story takes place, hence Ginny's fear of the Cherokee.

After this story, in 1838, many Cherokee were forced to move to Oklahoma along the Trail of Tears. A remnant remained in North Carolina and became the Eastern Band of the Cherokee, a federally recognized group committed to celebrating their culture.

The Tuscarora in North Carolina: *In the 17th century, the Tuscarora were considered a powerful and well-developed tribe of the Carolina coastlands. The arrival of more and more settlers caused conflict that culminated in the early 18th century's Tuscarora Wars.*

When the warfare concluded in 1713, the Tuscarora were forced to a reservation. Those who could not agree to reservation life moved north and joined the Five Nations of the Iroquois, becoming their Sixth Nation.

Over the next decades, other groups of Tuscarora families decided to join their kin in the north. This migration lasted until 1803. In this story, our Tuscarora native is making ready to depart for the north.

A remnant of the Tuscarora remained in eastern NC and struggled to maintain their identity. None of those remaining groups are officially recognized as Tuscarora bands.

5 – The Campfire

Not a dozen paces from the foot of the oak, the tracks blurred into nothing, and the only clue I had to follow was the general direction of the disturbed snow. I sighted a tall birch that lay along that bearing. I drew the leather cord of my hood tight against the wind and walked toward that tree.

The way was silent other than the rattle of dried leaves that still clung to their branches. My face and hands were numb, but there was the occasional taste of salt from my tears. The forest blurred into a gray mass, but the tall birch stood above the canopy, its branches silhouetted against the lighter clouds.

Then, I smelled something—meat cooking. Was it just my imagination—the power of suggestion spurred by my talk with Oat or maybe by the grackle I followed? Was the spirit of Cheenuh leading me through the woods? Papa would call such thoughts a fantasy, but there was little choice other than to keep walking. The smell grew stronger, and soon, I saw the glow of a campfire.

Warm fire. Warm feet. Food, be it warm or not. The mere chance of food and warmth was enough to drive me on, no matter what I found around that fire. I rushed forward, and when I could see the camp, there was Joe.

'Twas my instinct to call out to him, but Joe lay alone in the camp, as still as death. His head rested against a fallen oak log. A cord was wrapped around a branch jutting from that log, each end tethering one of Joe's hands. His coonskin cap lay beside a bedroll across the camp, and the butt of a long gun was just visible under the covering.

I moved to go to my brother, but movement in the tree branches stopped me. A man passed between two poplar saplings at the edge of the camp. I ducked back into the shadows as he moved in my direction. A black cloth wrapped like a bandage around his hair, and a bear tooth necklace fell away from his neck as he lay down the bow and water pouch he carried. I held my breath as he moved closer to me and sat on a log by the fire opposite my brother. At his feet lay a hatchet—Joe's hatchet.

The man studied my brother but did not move to help him. He opened his water pouch, and when he tipped his head back to drink his fill, the scarf fell from his head. A long, braided topknot started from his crown, and the plait of white and black strands trailed down his back. Indian. Cherokee were the only natives we ever saw in these parts. Legends told in the tavern said they were killers, and I had seen first-hand the result of their scalping on our neighbor, Mrs. Brank.

My brother was wounded. His rescue was up to me. But, if this old man got the better of Joe, how could I stand up to him? I had a knife, but I wasn't up to fighting with one. Papa's words echoed: *Pay attention to what's around you.* Besides the knife, I had only sticks and stones from the forest and the leather drawstring on my cloak.

6 - The Stranger

I sat in the shadows, still as a mouse, studying Joe for any sign of life. My brother moaned, and I stifled a gasp. He tried to sit up, but the cord held him fast, and he fell back against the log. On a second try, he settled for propping himself up on his elbows. There was little play in the cord, but he pulled the slack to one side. 'Twas enough for Joe to reach the knot on his head.

The Indian picked up his pouch and handed it to Joe. "Water," he said.

Joe shook his head, but that set him to moaning again. The man bent over to force the spout to my brother's lips. Joe took a sip, then kept drinking till the pouch was dry, and he pulled one elbow to the top of the log.

"Joe," he said, pointing to himself. Then he pointed to the man and said, "thank you," before his arm dropped and Joe's head fell to the crook of his elbow.

The stranger took the pouch and disappeared between the saplings. I followed to see where he went and to gauge how long there was before the captor's return. The filtered light from the moon and fire showed the path to the creek to be steep, rocky, and much too short for me to have time to rescue Joe.

I crept back through the shadows.

"Joe!"

My brother turned his head toward me and then winced as he snapped it back.

"Shh," he hissed, his eyes on his captor's path. "Go home."

"I don't know how," I whispered, then ducked back again as I heard the Indian returning.

I could barely make out the silhouette of the man as he passed through his gateway of saplings that led to the camp. He set the full water pouch beside him as he tended his roasting rabbit.

Those young trees covered me from the firelight as I removed the drawstrings from my cloak and set to work. I set the trap and slipped to my original spot, waiting for an opportunity to save my brother.

"Joe," my brother repeated, pointing to himself. Then he pointed to the stranger who spoke a name that sounded something like 'Clay.'

Joe pointed at the bear tooth. "Yonah?" he asked.

That was the one Cherokee word Joe and I both knew. Our friend Yonah was named 'bear' by his Cherokee captors.

"Bear," he replied. "Ocheereh"

"Not Cherokee?" my brother asked.

"Eat," Clay said, offering Joe part of his supper.

Joe shook his head, *no*. "Those are *my* rabbits. You took 'em from my gums by the river."

Clay looked at the rabbit on his fire spit and looked back at Joe. With a chuckle, he asked, "You brand rabbits here?"

The man's English was good enough to make a joke, but a jab at Joe only fueled his temper. Tied down or not, my brother was ready to blow. There was no holding him back, even trussed up like a hog.

With his eyes flashing and steel jaw set, he said, "No, we *do not* brand rabbits here, but these are *my* woods, and them's *my* rabbits. You took 'em, and you pointed that gun at me. I fell out of that mistletoe tree because of you, and now I'm tied up in your camp. You ain't gonna get away with that."

Clay chewed his rabbit slowly. He spoke no more, but his eyes never left Joe. Once the rabbit was eaten and his bones in the fire, the stranger stood in front of Joe, one hand on the knife in his belt, and poured the water at his feet. Joe's eyes narrowed. "You let me go, or I'll have every man in Burke County after you. They're already looking for you."

A growling scream nearby drew our attention to the woods. Three heads turned at once. 'Twas the panther. *Had it been stalking me? Oh, no! That sock I dropped.*

Joe sat up as high as he could. "Let me loose," he shouted.

Clay grabbed his gun and ran into the woods. Before he could aim, he fell over the trip string I tied between the saplings. *What a time for a plan of mine to work.* Clay cried out, and as he tumbled down the rocky path to the stream, branches snapped, and the rocks under the snow smacked into each other—and into Clay, too. The gun went off as the stranger's surprised yell went silent.

Time was short. I rushed into the campfire and cut the cord that held Joe, and he dashed for the hatchet.

A growl sounded from the western darkness, and I turned toward the sound. Yellow eyes grew larger as the great cat approached us. I shifted to the right, and so did those eyes. I froze, praying to God that Joe could reach that hatchet.

The lion was close enough to pounce. A low growl—a menacing rumble—sounded as the wide, tan head lowered for the spring. No doubt he could smell my fear. He crouched. I wanted to close my eyes, but even my eyelids were frozen in fear.

"Yeoowl" The cat screamed as a knife—Clay's knife—pierced its neck. As the beast spun to take on his attacker, Joe's hatchet drove into the cat's skull, and the panther fell dead in the woods.

"Thanks to God," I whined. "Let's go home."

"We can't go yet—not without seeing to Clay."

"Seeing to Clay?" I gasped. "Is your head still addled? Let's get out of here."

Joe could stand, but Clay had collapsed at the top of the rocky slope. He groaned as we pulled him to the fire. The old Indian was warmer there, but he was unconscious. Joe and I could do little for his wounds.

"His head looks worse than yours does, Joe."

My brother nodded. "Reckon the fall give him that knotted noggin and the twisted ankle, too. 'Tis a miracle he got up that hill in time to save us."

"Can we go home now?" I asked.

"What happened to all that Christmas charity you were talking about, Ginny?"

"Well, what are we going to do with him?"

"We will have to think of something. Watch him while I fetch his gun."

I moved into the shadows of the camp so that the man would not see me if he opened his eyes. If he couldn't see me, he probably couldn't scalp me. I kept my eye on him, though.

He didn't move. There was no sound. Was he breathing? I moved a few inches more so I could see his stony, pale face. Was he dead? Had I killed him? I was relieved when a finger twitched, and he sighed the softest of groans. I dared move closer and studied his face in the firelight.

The Indian resting in the camp was not the fearsome warrior from my nightmares. He was a wounded man lying by the fire, just as Joe had been only moments ago. His breath was shallow, and his head swollen from the fall. "Twas the Christmas season, but this man was not having a merry Christmas. Instead of bringing him cheer, I brought him to harm and led a panther to his camp. Joe was right. Clay had saved our lives, and what had I done for him?

At this moment, he had no one but me to care for him. I'd be his guardian. I listened for sounds of danger that threatened our safety, but I heard only the hinge-like squeak of a grackle that circled the fire and landed on the water pouch. When I shooed the bird away, I discovered enough water to wash Clay's head with my scarf.

The Indian roused once, but after a quick look around, he moaned and closed his eyes again.

"We can't leave him here," I told Joe upon his return. "The fire will go out. People die sleeping in the snow."

Joe nodded. "Yes, even if he did point a gun at me, he saved our lives, too."

The grackle returned and lit on Clay's shoulder.

"We're going to need the sled," I said.

7 – Oat Fogel to the Rescue

Once we made Clay as comfortable as we could, Joe and I headed back to the oak tree where our greenery still lay strewn around the sled. There was a surprise there, too. Oat Fogel stood studying the spilled boughs under the light of the lantern he carried. Father's horse, Chester, stood by as a silent witness.

"Here you are at last," Oat smiled.

"Oat? Thank God you're here." The sight of him brought tears that turned to ice on my cheeks. "How? ... You were spending time with Cheenuh...?"

"Cheenuh is here. Haven't you heard the screech of the grackle?" he said.

"Your father lost his children. He wanted to set the entire company of visitors to find you, but I convinced him to let me have a try first. I promised him I'd bring you home, and he believed I'd do it. That gunshot was a blessing, though. What happened to the gun?"

"'Twas Clay who fired the shot," Joe said.

I wrapped as much of the greenery as I could into my apron, and we tied that to the sled. "I guess we'll have to tie the stranger in there, too."

"Where is this stranger?" Oat asked.

We led Oat back to the campfire where the old peddler helped load the patient and his pack of belongings, and under the light of his lantern, he recognized an old friend. "'Tis no stranger you found. This man is my kin," Oat said.

"You're kin to Clay?" I asked.

"Are you sure his name is Clay?" Oat asked. "Could he have said, Akweh?"

"Akweh? That's a name?" Joe asked.

"'Tis a Tuscarora word," Oat replied. "It means deer, and that is the name of my wife's brother—Akweh, the deer."

Even with Joe's sore head and my frozen feet, we plodded behind Oat as he led the way back to our farm. Chester trudged under the load of the sled carrying Oat's old friend—a stranger who risked his own life to save my brother and me. When the lanterns of home shown through the trees, we forgot the difference between strangers, and we quickened our pace toward the light.

8 – Joe's Story

At the news of our return, Father and his callers found even more cheer than rum punch could bring. Mother and my sisters cried and hugged us till we thought we would smother, but they soon turned to the care of Akweh. Mary Jane brought her herbs and remedies, and Mother made sure we had our fill of the roast turkey and venison as well as the yams, puddings, and cakes on the tavern table.

Once we were warm, full, and healthier, Joe and I carried extra bedding to Oat's camp. The two old friends preferred an evening of remembrance to our tavern party, but before Joe and I left the camp, Oat and I heard the story of my brother's first meeting with our new friend.

"How's your head, Joe?" Akweh asked.

Joe pushed his hat back far enough to rub the knot on his head. "Not too bad. Yours?"

"How did you hurt your head, Joe?" Oat asked.

Patricia Cooper Baker

"Did you fall out of the tree trying to hold on to your mistletoe?" I asked.

"No, that ain't exactly it," my brother replied, "There was plenty of mistletoe on that tree, but I had to climb high to get to it. My hatchet banged against my knee more than once, and the bark scraped it, too. Even so, I made it to the longest limb where there was a big harvest."

"I hacked off a few branches and dropped them to the sled then climbed to a higher branch, staying near the trunk for safety. I gathered as I climbed higher and higher, till I figured I might spot you, Ginny. There was no sign of you in the dark woods but huddled near a campfire in the distance a man was roasting rabbits." He pointed to Akweh.

"I itched to clamber down and get a hold of that poacher, but there'd be folks willing to pay a penny or two for mistletoe. I dasn't leave it in the tree without harvesting the branch I was on before going after the thief."

"I reset your traps, and by now, they are full again," Akweh said.

Joe continued, "Getting them blasted sprigs off'n the tree took some hacking and chopping. That, plus keeping my footing in the tree, took all the focus I could muster. After a while, though, between my smacks of the hatchet, I heard scraping and tapping nearby. *Dadgummit!* Below me, a man was fiddlin' with my sled and riflin' through my mistletoe."

"I thought you might know where I could find Oat Fogel," Akweh chuckled. "That's why I shouted up to you."

"He shouted, and I saw he had a gun. That didn't stop me. I called out, 'Are you the feller who stole my rabbits?' Then he raised that gun to point right at me."

"I didn't point my gun at you; I was just holding it while I looked for you," Akweh said.

"My hatchet stuck in the tree's bark, but I grabbed ahold and gave it a big yank. Truth is I yanked too hard and lost my balance. Down from that tree, I came, tumbling, twisting, waving my axe like a wild man, and yelling to beat the band. My behind struck snow, and the fall jarred the hatchet from my hand, but I jumped up and took to wrestlin' that man."

Akweh chuckled, "'Twas a fair match."

"We wallered around till we rolled over on that sled and got tangled up. I tripped over the runners and struck my head on the oak tree. The next thing I remember is waking up tied to a log."

"I didn't want you to run away before I could talk to you. Besides, you needed looking after," Akweh replied.

"Well, things turned out better than I thought they would, I can promise you that," Joe admitted.

"It turned out better than I hoped, too," Akweh said, turning to Oat. "I had given up on finding Oat Fogel. To think I came looking for you and 'twas you who found me, instead."

"'Tis a great joy to see you, friend, but why did you pick such a time for a visit?" Oat asked.

The smile left Akweh's face as he replied, "Our people grow fewer and fewer. Six of us will travel north before the next planting. We will join our kin who live among the Iroquois now. But Cheenuh came to me in a dream, insisting I must say farewell to you first. She wanted me to give you this."

Akweh opened his pack and removed a cedar flute engraved with a deer carving. "She said you need it more than I do."

Tears slipped down Oat's cheeks as his fingers ran over the smooth wooden flute carved by his beloved. The old man grasped his brother-in-law by the hand, and the two of them spent the night telling stories of old times and their love for Cheenuh.

9 – Party at the Tavern

Dozens of friends and neighbors joined our family for the festivities that night. Those who felt inclined danced to the music of Father's fiddle and David's accompaniment on the spoons. Charlie Holberry joined in with his willow flute, and Grace McDowell strummed along on her lap harp.

Ladies sang carols, old men told stories, and kisses were stolen from under the mistletoe by those of all ages. Our little tavern must have glowed as brightly as the Christmas star with all the merriment we made.

The very last of the partiers to leave were Colonel Charles McDowell and his wife, Grace.

"Come shooting with us on the Twelfth day," Colonel Charles said. "I promise you a slice of Grace's black cake. There's none better in the state, I vow."

***

At breakfast the next morning, Oat and Akweh joined our table. Before the old Tuscarora left us, Oat gave his friend a list of good trading men who would be of help as he set off on his journey. When the farewells were complete, Oat Fogel returned to his camp whistling a Christmas tune.

"Well, you didn't find any rabbits for Oat," Joe said, "but somehow he found his cheer anyway."

"'Tis like Father says, good works attempted turn into good works done, even if it is done differently from how you intended," I said. "Who knows what good will follow? After all, 'tis only the start of the Christmas season."

A grackle screeched and flitted from tree to tree, following Oat toward his camp.

"You know, Joe," I said, "'tis the season for miracles. Recheck those traps. I suspect Oat will find his rabbit after all."

1780's Christmas Gifts

Christmas in the 18th century was not a child's holiday. The parties, hunts, and dances were better fare for the adults. However, children were sometimes recipients of gifts, and the visitors and extra treats surely delighted them.

Gift-giving in those days was not an exchange of presents between friends, or equals, but it was more a charitable thought to those less fortunate or of lesser social standing. Children fell into that category. Fathers may give gifts to their children, but children would not think of making gifts for their parents.

Gifts may pass from plantation owner to farmhand, from the rich to the less fortunate, from master to apprentice, or even from slave master to the slave. These gifts were usually small tokens such as cash tips or small amounts of sweets. Slaves were sometimes given candy and rum to enjoy on their days off from work.

Wealthy families could afford to be more elaborate. In 1759, George Washington gave Martha's children gifts, including a bird on a bellows, a Prussian Soldier, a grocer's shop, and a tea set.

Holiday Events in Modern Burke County

Historic Burke Holiday Tour

The **Historic Burke Foundation** offers an annual tour of historic homes and churches around Burke County. The oldest home, The McDowell House, was built in 1812, the others are from the 19th and early 20th centuries.

The Tour is offered on a Saturday in early December, and at each stop on the tour, history, traditions, and architectural significance are highlighted. Each home is decorated for the holidays, and at some stops, refreshments and entertainment are provided.

Contact **Historic Burke Foundation** for more information.

Morganton Winter Carnival

The holiday season kicks off in Morganton with the November **Winter Carnival**. A focal point of the carnival is lighting the **Memorial Tree**. Carnival attendees may dedicate a light to the memory of a loved one, and when the lights of the tree fire up, so do the decorations around the old Court House and along the streets of the town. Then the Carnival begins.

Carriage rides, visits to Santa, marshmallow roasts, face painting are all part of the fun. Santa, the carriage rides, and light displays continue throughout the holiday season.

Town Parades

Holiday parades are held in several county towns, including Valdese and Drexel, as well as Morganton.

J. Iverson Riddle Decoration and Parade

A big part of Burke County's holidays back in the 50s and early 60s was driving through the holiday displays on the grounds of Broughton Hospital. In 1963, when Western Carolina Center was built, the displays moved to those grounds, and that tradition continues.

The center, now called J. Iverson Riddle Developmental Center, begins as early as July to prepare over fifty displays to delight visitors and residents. The work is primarily done by volunteers, residents, and the Creative Therapy Department staff at the center.

Each year 10,000-15,000 visitors view the festive decorations and animated displays. There is also a parade through the grounds to highlight the holiday season.

Waldensian Heritage Trail of Faith Christmas Lights

In 1893, twenty-nine Waldensians fled religious persecution and came to Burke County to settle in the wilderness. They struggled and persevered to build the town of Valdese.

One hundred years later, Jim Jacumin, a Waldensian descendant, was inspired to tell the story of his ancestors at a site called The Trail of Faith.

This Trail, well worth a visit at any time of year, adds to Christmas cheer with a light display throughout the holiday season.

Contact **Waldensian Trail of Faith Organization** for more information.

References

DeSimone, D. (2019). Colonial Williamsburg. *Another Look at Christmas in the 18th Century.* Retrieved 2019, from. https://www.history.org/almanack/life/christmas/hist_anotherlook.cfm

Gill, Jr., H.B. (2019). Colonial Williamsburg. *Christmas in Colonial Virginia.* Retrieved 2019, from https://www.history.org/almanack/life/christmas/hist_inva.cfm

Glasse, H. (1747). *The Art of Cookery Made Plain and Easy.* England: L. Wangford

Olmert, M. (2019). Colonial Williamsburg. *Christmas Earnest and Game Ball.* Retrieved 2019: https://www.history.org/almanack/life/christmas/hist_games.cfm

Pelton, R. (2003). *Revolutionary War Period Cookery.* United States: Infinity Publishing.com.

Phifer, Jr., E. (1982). *Burke: The History of a North Carolina County.* North Carolina: Edward W. Phifer, Jr.

Powers, E.L. (1995). Colonial Williamsburg. *Christmas Customs.* Retrieved 2019, from https://www.history.org/almanack/life/xmas/customs.cfm

Snyder, R. (2019). Colonial Williamsburg. *History of Chocolate: Chocolate in the American Colonies.* Retrieved 2019. https://www.history.org/history/teaching/enewsletter/volume9/jan11/featurearticle.cfm

Various Contributors. (2019, March 7). Wikipedia. *Shinty.* Retrieved June 17, 2019, from https://en.wikipedia.org/w/index.php?title=Shinty&oldid=886575923

About the Author

Patricia Cooper Baker, a descendant of the Cooper family fictionalized in this novel, was born in Burke County, NC, surrounded by Cooper relatives living on properties that had been in the family from near Revolutionary War times. Burke County records have suffered the ravages of time, natural disaster, and war. Even with limited and challenging data, Patricia enjoys researching and creating stories from the few clues left about her family in the state, county, and colonial records.

www.ingramcontent.com/pod-product-compliance
Lightning Source LLC
Chambersburg PA
CBHW070650130626
46555CB00006B/2798